This edition published by Parragon Books Ltd in 2014

Parragon Books Ltd
Chartist House
15–17 Trim Street
Bath BA1 1HA, UK
www.parragon.com

Written by Catherine Hapka
Illustrated by the Disney Storybook Art Team

ISBN 978-1-4723-8214-6

Printed in China

Disney

Sofia
the First

Holiday
in
Enchancia

Written by

Catherine Hapka

Illustrated by the

Disney Storybook
Art Team

PaRragon

Bath · New York · Cologne · Melbourne · Delhi
Hong Kong · Shenzhen · Singapore · Amsterdam

I'm Sofia

and I am one excited

princess!

This will be my first Wassailia holiday in the castle
and I don't want to miss a second of it!

I'm used to spending a quiet Wassailia with Mum.

But James and Amber say that here in the castle, Wassailia is really **different.**

There's **tonnes** of food . . .

a **giant** Wassailia willow . . .

a **fancy** Wassailia candle . . .

and lots and **lots** of presents.

"Happy Wassailia, Amber!"
I say.

"It will be if I get that
unicorn I've been asking for,"
she replies.

Just then, my mum comes in.
"Where's Dad?" James asks.

Mum says he's out
on urgent royal business with Baileywick.
"He'll be back in time for the party, though."

While I wait for
Dad to get back, I go to
visit **Minimus**, my
favourite flying horse.
But when I get to the
stable, all the other
horses have colds.

Minimus is okay, though.
He tells me that he's glad to spend the
holiday with me.

It has started snowing again by the time I get back to the castle and Dad's still not home!

"Shouldn't he be back by now?" I ask.
Amber nods. "It's almost time for the party."

Mum asks Constable Myles
to look for the king.

"I want to go, too!" I say.
"If she's going, I'm going," says James.
"Why don't we all go?" my mum suggests.
"We can take the flying coach."

Minimus is the only **flying** horse
healthy enough to pull the coach.

"Minimus can do it!" I say.
"I'm not so sure about that," Minimus mutters.

As our coach takes off,
I see Clover, Robin and Mia hop on to the back.
I guess they want to help find my dad, too!

Soon the coach is **flying** over the road.
I look down and spot the royal horses.
But there's no sign of the royal coach!

"The storm is getting worse,"
Constable Myles says. "We need to turn round."
I shake my head. "We can't go back until
we find Dad!"

Then the forest disappears in a flurry of snow.
It's a blizzard!

Poor Minimus. I can tell he's
really scared, but he lands the
coach safely.

Constable Myles wants everyone to
wait inside the coach until the storm passes.
But Mum knows how **worried** I am about
Minimus, so she lets me check on him.

"What are we going to do, Minimus?" I say.
"We have to find Dad!"

Suddenly,

my amulet starts to glow ...
and Princess Aurora appears!

"Princess Aurora!" I cry.

"Did you come to help us?"

"It's not my help you need," Aurora replies.

"I could always count on my animal

friends to help me through tough times,

and so can you."

When I see Clover, Robin and Mia,
I think that **Aurora** might be
right: maybe my animal friends
can help! I ask them to gather the
creatures of the woods to help
search for the king.

Pretty soon, a message spreads
through the whole forest:

We must find the king!

Then they see him!

Before long, Robin and Mia
return with good news.
"We found him!"

Amber
looks puzzled.

"What are

your birds

doing here?"

Uh-oh. I can understand what they're saying,
but everyone else just hears chirping.

I have to think fast.
"Um ... I think they're trying to tell us something!"
I convince everyone to follow the birds.

Minimus pulls the coach through the snow
until it comes to a cosy little wood cabin.

We knock on the door.
Guess who's inside. . . ?

Dad!

"How did you find me?" he asks us.
"It's a Wassailia miracle!" I say, giving him a
big hug. "But how did you end up here?"

Dad admits that his urgent royal business was actually going to town to find presents for us. But the road back to the castle was icy and the royal coach got stuck in the snow!

"Luckily," says Baileywick,
"this kind woodsman found us and invited us
to take shelter in his cabin with his family."

"This is what the holidays are all about,"
Dad says. "Spending time with your loved ones."

I look at all the presents my dad has for us
and I know what to do. "Happy Wassailia!" I say,
giving my presents to the woodsman's children.

Then I help Mum and Dad light the Wassailia candle.

Well, my first Wassailia with my new family isn't exactly like I expected. But we are spending it together ... and that makes it the

best holiday ever!

The End